U0065154

David's First Party

大維的驚奇派對

Coleen Reddy　著

倪靖、郜欣、王平　繪

蘇秋華　譯

三民書局

For Gareth

Thank you for everything.

致 *Gareth*

感謝你為我所做的一切

On Saturday morning, David woke up and yawned loudly. He felt good because it was Saturday; it was the weekend. That meant there was no school. He could lie in bed and wake up whenever he wanted. He usually waited until he was really hungry and his stomach grumbled before he woke up. It felt really good to just lie in bed and relax. Suddenly, his smile dropped off his face and he rushed out of bed.

"Oh no!" he said, "Today is Amy's birthday party. What am I going to wear? I don't have any cool clothes like the others. Everyone will laugh at my stupid, cheap clothes."

2

He quickly ran into the bathroom to wash his face.
Suddenly, there was a loud scream from the bathroom.
David's mother came rushing up the stairs.

She tried to open the door but it was locked. "David, David, open the door! Are you okay? What happened?" she asked. She was worried. She thought David had hurt himself. He had screamed very loudly.

Maybe he had fallen in the bathtub. Maybe he was bleeding. Something terrible had happened.

She could hear him moaning softly.

"I'm okay," he said unhappily.

"Well, what happened?" his mother asked.

"I have THREE new pimples," he groaned.

"Three new pimples," his mother said, "that's why you screamed?"

"They're NOT just three pimples; they're BIG, UGLY pimples that make me look ugly. How can I go to Amy's party looking like this?" he said.

"David! I can't believe you screamed because you saw pimples on your face. You're thirteen years old; pimples are normal at your age. It's not a big deal. It's not the end of the world. I thought you were hurt; you sounded like you were dying," she said.

"You don't understand. It is a big deal," he said.

"I've heard enough of this. Hurry up! Breakfast is almost ready. I'm making your favorite blueberry pancakes," she said.

"I don't want blueberry pancakes," he said, "I want to be handsome and have expensive clothes."

He took a shower and went downstairs to eat breakfast.

His dad and mom were already eating.

"Good morning," his father said.

"Good morning," David mumbled.

Five minutes later, David decided that it was time to speak to his dad. His dad was always in a good mood on Saturday mornings.

He smiled sweetly and asked, "Dad, may I have some money to go shopping for clothes, please?"

"Your mother bought new clothes for you last week," his dad said.

"Yes, but I want to choose my own clothes. I'm thirteen years old," David said.

"What's wrong with the clothes your mother bought you?" his dad asked.

"They're not cool. They make me look like a geek! I need to wear something awesome to the party tonight," David said.

"How can you say that?" his mother said. "You're so ungrateful!"

"Pretty please, Dad. It's my first party," David said.

"You can have $50!" his dad said.

"But I can't buy anything with $50," David whined.

"What are you talking about?" his father asked. His dad was angry now so David decided to keep quiet.

"I'm sorry. Thank you for the $50," David said.

"You must use it carefully because I won't give you more money until next month," his father said.

David didn't say anything. Everybody ate their pancakes in silence.

After breakfast, David went to the shopping mall. He knew exactly what he wanted and he knew exactly where to find it. He had wanted them ever since he saw Jason wearing them at school. Jason was very popular and dressed well. David always wanted what Jason had. This time it was a pair of jeans. They weren't any old pair of jeans. They were the new Levi's. They were black. David wanted them more than anything. He imagined himself wearing them to Amy's party and looking so cool that all the girls would want to talk to him.

The jeans were $59 but David used his savings to fill in the $9 that his father didn't give him. He would have no money to spend on anything for the next three weeks but he didn't mind. The new Levi's were worth it.

David went into the store and tried on the pair of jeans. They were a baggy fit. He wanted to buy a pair of jeans that were really loose. Jason's jeans were so baggy and loose that you could see his underpants. Of course, that was okay because they were "CK" underpants. David chose the pair of jeans he wanted and after paying for them, he went home.

At home, his mom wanted to see what he had bought, but David said that she could see them later when he was wearing them. He was in a rush because it was 5 p.m. and the party started at 7 p.m. He had only two hours to get ready. There were lots of things he had to do.

Next, he looked at his pimples very, very closely. He couldn't go to the party with pimples. There was only one thing left to do. He had to pop them. His mother always told him not to pop them because they left marks on his face. But the party was more important.

"Ouch!" said David as he popped his pimples. It hurt a little.

Then he got dressed. He put on his new jeans and then looked at himself in the mirror. Baggy, very baggy. You could almost see his underpants. He hoped no one saw his underpants because he didn't have "CK" underpants but ugly blue and red underpants that his mom always bought.

Finally, he sneaked into his parents' bedroom and picked up his father's aftershave. He opened the bottle and used some on his neck and chest. But he used too much. It made him sneeze.

David was ready to go to the party. He went downstairs. His parents looked at his new jeans with a funny look on their faces.

"Son," said his father, "aren't those jeans a little too big for you?"

David groaned. His parents were so old. They didn't know anything.

"No, Dad," he said, "they're supposed to look like this. It's the new fashion. Everybody wears jeans like this."

He walked up to the front door and rang the bell. No one answered so he rang the bell again.

"Maybe the music's so loud that they can't hear me," he thought.

Someone opened the door. It
was Amy. She was wearing a sweat suit, which was a
strange choice of clothing for her own birthday party.

大維的驚奇派對

星期六早上大維醒過來，打了個大大的呵欠。今天是星期六，他感覺棒極了，因為是週末，用不著趕著上學，他可以賴在床上，什麼時候起床都行。通常他會一直賴到肚子餓得咕咕叫才起來。懶洋洋躺在床上的感覺實在好好。但就在這時，他的笑容突然消失了，趕緊跳下床。

「慘了啦！」他自言自語：「今天是愛玫的生日派對，我要穿什麼呢？我不像別人一樣有時髦的衣服可以穿，穿一套難看的便宜貨鐵定會被大家笑死。」

他迅速衝到浴室裡洗臉。突然，浴室裡傳出一聲慘叫，媽媽急忙衝上樓來。

她想把門打開，可是門卻鎖住了。

她憂心忡忡地問：「大維！大維！開門哪！你還好嗎？發生什麼事了？」

她以為大維受傷了，不然怎麼會叫得那麼淒厲，八成是在浴缸裡滑倒、流血了。總之，一定是發生了什麼不好的事情。她甚至可以聽到大維在浴室裡低聲呻吟。

浴室傳出大維悲慘的聲音：「我沒事。」

媽媽問：「究竟怎麼了？」

他喃喃地抱怨：「我新長了三顆痘子。」

「三顆痘子，」媽媽遲疑了一下：「這個就是你大叫的原因？」

大維說：「它們不只是三顆痘子，它們是又大又醜的三顆痘子，我變得好難看。妳叫我怎麼頂著這張臉去參加愛玫的派對？」

媽媽說：「天哪！大維，我真不敢相信你居然為了幾顆痘子叫成這樣。你今年十三歲了，長痘子是很正常，沒什麼大不了的，又不是世界末日。你叫得一副快死了的樣子，害我以為你受傷了。」

(p.1〜p.7)

大維回她：「妳不懂啦，這很嚴重。」

媽媽說：「夠了，別再說了。動作快一點！早餐已經快好了，今天是你最愛吃的藍莓煎餅。」

「我才不稀罕藍莓煎餅，」大維咕噥著：「我只想變得帥一點，然後有昂貴的衣服可以穿。」

洗完澡，大維才下樓吃早餐。爸媽都已經在吃了。

爸爸對大維說：「早啊。」

大維含糊地回答：「早。」

五分鐘後，大維下定決心對爸爸開口，因為星期六早上爸爸的心情總是一級棒。

他堆起甜甜的笑容，然後問：「爸，你可不可以給我點錢去買衣服？拜託啦！」

(p.7～p.9)

爸爸卻說：「你媽媽上個禮拜不是才買新衣服給你嗎？」

大維說：「對啦，可是我想選自己要穿的衣服，我已經十三歲了。」

爸爸很納悶：「媽媽買給你的衣服有什麼不好？」

大維抱怨：「不夠酷，我穿起來像個怪胎！我希望今天晚上在派對上能穿得正一點。」

媽媽插口說：「大維，你怎麼講這種話？真是個不知感恩的孩子。」

大維才不管：「拜託求求你啦！爸爸，這是我第一次參加派對呢。」

爸爸說：「好吧，那我給你五十塊好了。」

大維哀叫說：「五十塊能買什麼？」

爸爸問：「你說什麼？」看爸爸一臉不高興的樣子，大維決定閉嘴。

他說：「對不起，謝謝你給我五十塊錢。」

爸爸說：「大維，你一定要省點花，因為一直到下個月，我都不會再給你半毛錢了。」

大維不再講話了。全家人靜靜地吃完煎餅。

37

(p.9～p.11)

吃完早飯後，大維直奔購物中心。他很清楚自己要的是什麼，也知道該上哪兒找。自從在學校看到杰生穿的那天起，他就一直想要一件。杰生是個萬人迷，穿著一向很正，而大維總是希望得到杰生擁有的一切。這次，他想要的是一條牛仔褲，可不是什麼破舊的牛仔褲喔，而是Levi's的新款黑色牛仔褲。這是大維在這世界上最想要的東西了。他想像自己穿上它，去參加愛玫的派對，看起來多酷啊，所有的女孩子都會想和他說話。牛仔褲是五十九元，因為爸爸給的錢不夠，大維還動用了自己儲蓄的九塊錢。花了這錢，接下來的三個禮拜，他是一毛錢也沒得花了，可是他並不在意。為了這條新款Levi's牛仔褲，一切都值得。大維走進店裡，試穿那條牛仔褲，穿起來鬆鬆垮垮的，正符合他的要求。杰生的牛仔褲就是又寬又大，大到內褲都露出來了，當然啦，露出來也無所謂，因為杰生穿的是「卡文‧克萊」的內褲。大維選好牛仔褲，付完錢後就回家了。

(p.13～p.15)

回到家，媽媽想看大維買了什麼，可是大維卻要媽媽等他待會兒穿上了再看，因為他在趕時間。現在已經五點了，派對是七點開始，他只剩兩個小時的時間可以準備，而要做的事實在太多。

首先，他沖了個澡，還洗了頭髮，用去他三十分鐘。接下來，他用吹風機把頭髮吹乾，花了十分鐘。等頭髮乾了，他又把一大堆髮膠往頭上抹，讓頭髮一根根豎起來，整顆頭活像隻豪豬，等頭髮弄好時已經六點了。之後，大維極其謹慎地看著自己的痘痘，他不能帶著痘痘去參加派對，因此現在只剩下一件事是他必須做的——把痘痘擠掉。媽媽一向告訴他痘痘千萬不能擠，否則會留下疤痕。可是比較起來派對更重要！

痘子被擠破時，大維忍不住「噢！」地一聲叫了出來，有點痛。然後他開始穿衣服。他穿上那條新買的牛仔褲，打量鏡中的自己。寬、鬆、垮，內褲都快露出來了。他希望不要有人看到自己的內褲，因為那不是「卡文·克萊」，他的內褲是媽媽買的，紅藍相間有夠醜。

（p.17～p.22）

最後，他偷偷溜進爸媽房間，拿起爸爸的刮鬍水，打開瓶子，拍了一點在自己的脖子和胸前。可是他倒太多了，忍不住開始打起噴嚏。

大維準備好要參加派對了，他走下樓，爸媽看到他的新牛仔褲，臉上浮現古怪的表情。

「兒子，」爸爸說：「你的牛仔褲會不會太大了點？」

大維嘀咕著，爸媽真是老古板，什麼都不懂。

他回答：「不會啊，爸爸，這條牛仔褲本來就這樣，是現在最流行的，大家都這樣穿。」

（p.23～p.25）

爸爸載大維到愛玫家。大維頭一次參加這麼「盛大」的生日派對，緊張得要命，胃液翻騰不已，他覺得有點想吐。

車子開到愛玫家，情況卻有點不對勁，居然連一輛車也沒有，附近也看不到半個人影，大維心想自己可能早到了。他下了車，爸爸就把車子開走了。

大維走到前門按了按門鈴，沒人回應，因此他又再按了一次。

他暗想：「會不會是音樂開得太大聲，聽不到鈴聲？」

終於有人來開門了，那個人正是愛玫，她身上穿的是運動服，在自己的生日派對上穿這種衣服好像有點怪。

大維笑著說：「愛玫，祝妳生日快樂，我是不是早到了？」

(p.26～p.30)

全新的大喜故事來囉！這回大喜又將碰上什麼？讓我們趕快來瞧瞧！

Anna Fienberg & Barbara Fienberg ／著　Kim Gamble ／繪　柯美玲・王盟雄／譯

大喜與奇妙鐘

哎呀呀！
村裡的奇妙鐘被河盜偷走了，
聰明的大喜
能幫村民們取回奇妙鐘嗎？

大喜與大臭蟲

可惡的大巨人！
不但吃掉人家的烤豬，
還吃掉人家的兒子。
大喜有辦法將巨人趕走嗎？

大喜與魔笛

糟糕！走了一群蝗蟲，
卻來了個吹笛人，
把村裡的孩子們都帶走了。
快來瞧瞧大喜是怎麼救回他們的！

樣的難題呢？

大喜與算命仙

大喜就要死翹翹了！？
這可不妙！
盧半仙提議的方法，
真的救得了大喜嗎？

大喜勇退惡魔

蜘蛛、蛇和老鼠！
惡魔們絞盡腦汁要逼大喜
說出公主的下落，
大喜要怎麼從惡魔手中逃脫呢？

大喜與寶鞋

大喜的表妹阿蓮失蹤了！
為了尋找阿蓮，
大喜穿上了飛天的寶鞋。
寶鞋究竟會帶他到哪裡去呢？

●中英對照●

探索英文叢書・中高級

波波 唸翻天系列

你知道可愛的小兔子也會 "碎碎唸" 嗎？
波波就是這樣。
他將要告訴我們什麼有趣的故事呢？

波波的復活節／波波的西部冒險記／波波上課記
我愛你，波波／波波的下雪天／波波郊遊去
波波打球記／聖誕快樂，波波／波波的萬聖夜

共 9 本，每本均附 CD

國家圖書館出版品預行編目資料

David's First Party:大維的驚奇派對／Coleen Reddy
著;倪靖,邰欣,王平繪;蘇秋華譯.－－初版一刷.
－－臺北市;三民,2002
　　面;公分--(愛閱雙語叢書. 青春記事簿系列)
中英對照
ISBN 957-14-3655-0　(平裝)

805

© **David's First Party**
　　　── 大維的驚奇派對

著作人　Coleen Reddy
繪　圖　倪靖　邰欣　王平
譯　者　蘇秋華
發行人　劉振強
著作財　三民書局股份有限公司
產權人　臺北市復興北路三八六號
發行所　三民書局股份有限公司
　　　　地址／臺北市復興北路三八六號
　　　　電話／二五○○六六○○
　　　　郵撥／○○○九九九八──五號
印刷所　三民書局股份有限公司
門市部　復北店／臺北市復興北路三八六號
　　　　重南店／臺北市重慶南路一段六十一號
初版一刷　西元二○○二年十一月
編　號　S 85616
定　價　新臺幣參佰伍拾元整
行政院新聞局登記證局版臺業字第○二○○號

　　有著作權·不准侵害

ISBN　957-14-3655-0　(平裝)

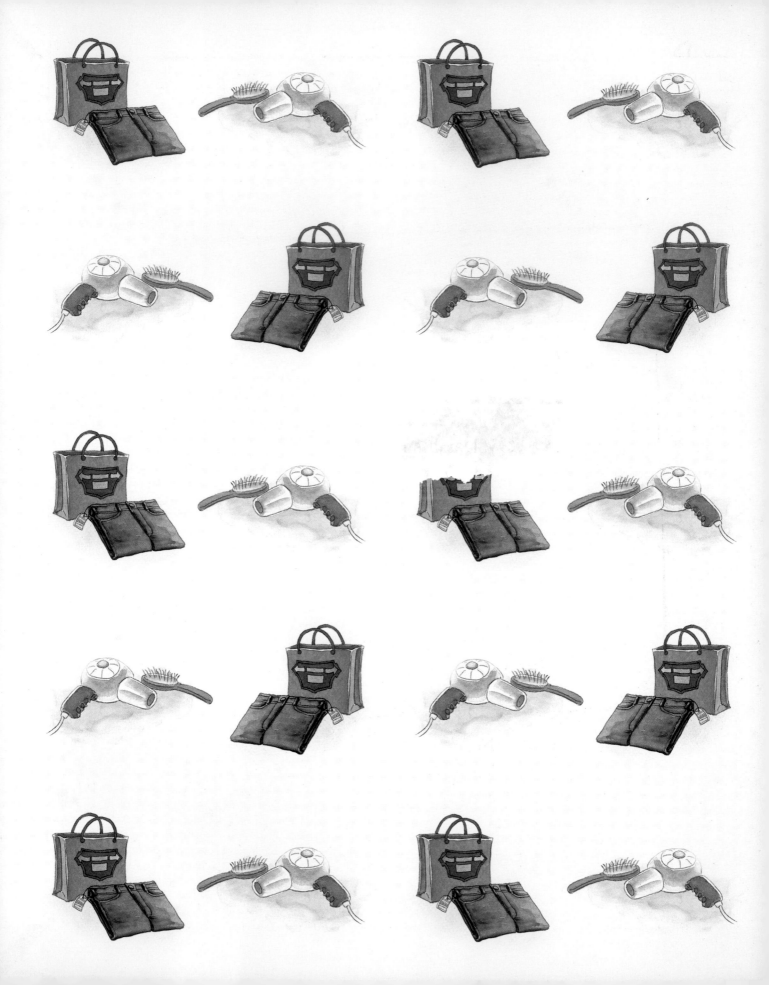